Chandra's Magic Light

For Vanessa — T. H.

Barefoot Books
294 Banbury Road
Oxford, OX2 7ED

Graphic design by Louise Millar, London
Reproduction by B & P International, Hong Kong
Printed in China on 100% acid-free paper
This book was typeset in Veljovic and Braganza
The illustrations were prepared in acrylic paint,
coloured pencils and collage.

Hardback ISBN 978-1-84686-492-6
Paperback ISBN 978-1-84686-865-8

British Cataloguing-in-Publication Data:
a catalogue record for this book
is available from the British Library

1 3 5 7 9 8 6 4 2

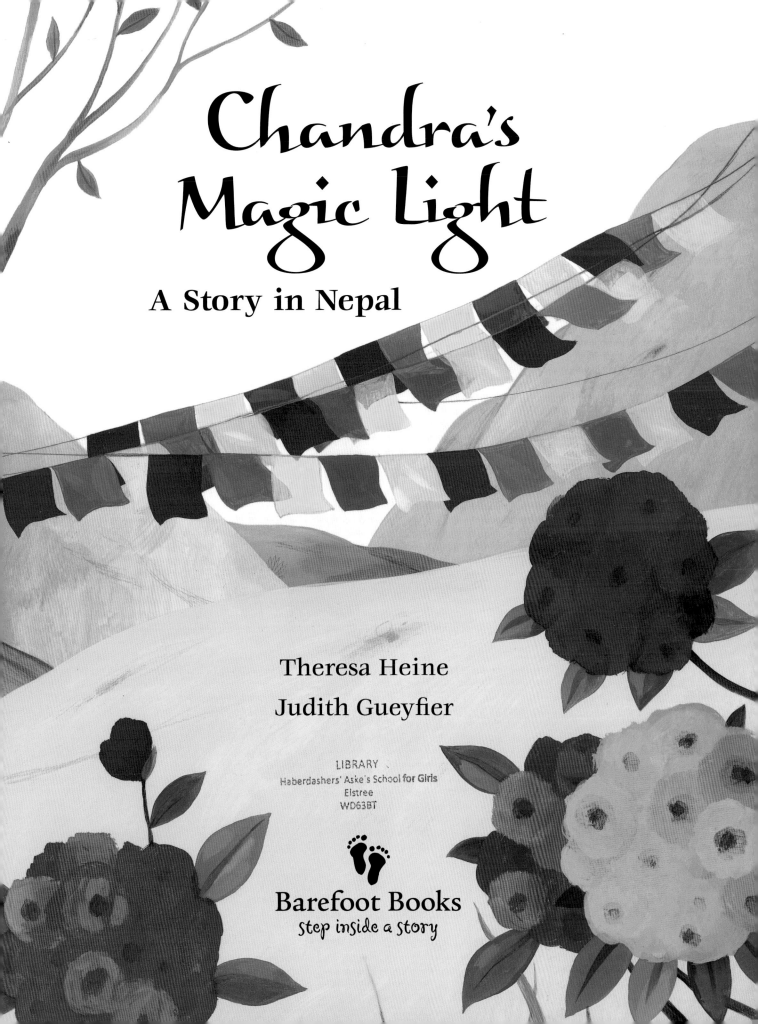

Chandra's Magic Light

A Story in Nepal

Theresa Heine

Judith Gueyfier

Barefoot Books
step inside a story

Chandra and Deena were at the market. It was dusty and noisy. Sacks full of herbs and spices were laid out on the ground, all the colours of the rainbow. Chandra closed her eyes and sniffed: ginger, garlic, coriander, cardamom, curry leaves. Her sister bought lentils, honey in a little cardboard box and something in a small paper package.

'What's that?' Chandra asked.

'It's a herb called *tulsi*,' Deena answered. 'Mother will make it into tea for Akash. It will help his cough. So will the honey.'

'Can we have a drink?' Chandra asked.
'I'm really thirsty.'

Deena counted out fifty paisa from her
little beaded purse.

'We'll share a cup of pomegranate juice,' she said.

Deena took a sip and then gave the rest to Chandra.
Chandra let the juice run slowly down her throat,
wet and cold and sweet.

Then she noticed a group of people clustered round
a man who was holding a strange lamp.

'It's all done by the sun, you see,' he was saying. 'The panel here gets power from the sun. The energy of the sun goes into these batteries and they light up the lamps. Over time, it will cost you less than all the kerosene you have to keep buying for your *tukis*. It's much healthier too — no more bad chests from smoke.'

'Getting rid of those smoky *tukis* would be a very good thing,' said a woman.

'Our *tuki* caught fire last week. They're very dangerous,' said her friend.

'Deena, let's buy a new sun *tuki*.' Chandra was jumping up and down. 'Then Akash's cough will get better.'

'I can't buy one without asking Father,' said Deena. 'And I don't have enough money. That sign says the lamps cost three thousand rupees each!'

'Let's go quickly and tell Father,' said Chandra, seizing Deena's hand.

The two girls hurried out of the market and back across the hills. They came to the rickety bridge over the river. Chandra held her big sister's hand very tightly. The river roared beneath them like a dragon as they walked carefully across the wet logs. Then they hurried down the path to their village.

Father was in the courtyard cutting firewood.

'Quickly, Father, you must come to the market,' Chandra panted.

Father dropped his axe. 'What has happened? Has there been an accident?'

'No, no,' said Chandra, her words spilling out all over the place. 'There's a man, a man in the market. He has a magic light! He catches the sun in it and makes it shine!'

Father frowned. 'Catching light from the sun? What's this nonsense, Chandra?'

'It's true, Father,' said Deena. 'But it isn't magic. The lamp gets light from the sun in the daytime and then it shines at night. It's called solar energy and it'll help Akash.'

Mother came out of the house with Akash.

'Did you get the *tulsi* and the honey?' she asked.

'Yes and there's a magic lamp and we won't need the kerosene anymore and Akash's cough will get better,' said Chandra. 'But please come now or they will all be gone.'

Father looked cross. 'Stop, Chandra. We have no money for magic lights. Go and help your mother. And Deena, you can help me with the wood.'

The next morning, they went to fetch water from the river. Outside a neighbour's house they saw a small, shiny object lying out in the sun. Chandra clutched Deena's arm. 'It's the lamp, the lamp from the market!'

With water slopping everywhere, they hurried home.

'Let me explain this time,' said Deena when they arrived. 'Mahesh Saud, by the river, has the lamp we were telling you about,' she called out. 'Come and see!'

Father came to look and Mahesh Saud showed him how the lamp worked. But Father's face was downcast when he came back.

'It's a solar *tuki*,' he said. 'It works well, but it costs three thousand rupees. We don't need to pay it all at once, but we do need five hundred rupees for a deposit and I don't have any money left this month.'

'We can earn some money,' said Chandra, as Deena milked the goat. 'We still have three weeks holiday from school.'

'I could make necklaces and bracelets out of beads and sell them in the market,' said Deena. 'But we have no money to buy the beads and there is already a stall selling bracelets.'

Chandra jumped up. 'I know, Deena! We could sell flowers!'

Deena and Chandra got up very early the
next morning. They climbed high into the hills
and picked big bunches of wild rhododendrons:
crimson, pink and cream.

They took the flowers down to the market and sat on the ground next to the spice stall. The spice lady gave them tins with water to put the flowers in. It was so early that the market was still very quiet.

'Tell me a story, Deena,' said Chandra. 'Tell me about Surya and Chandra.'

'When morning comes, the great sun god, Surya, rides out of the sky in his chariot,' said Deena. 'He has seven horses, each one a colour of the rainbow. He rules the sky all through the day.'

'Then what happens?' Chandra asked.

'Then it's evening and time for the moon to rise. Chandra, the moon god, rides into the sky in his chariot, pulled by seven geese.'

'What colour are the geese?' asked Chandra.

'They are pure white,' said Deena. 'Like the snow on the top of the highest mountain. They are as big as horses and their wings are as wide as the river. On each side of the chariot are two archers. They shoot arrows into the sky to drive away the darkness.'

'Is the moon god very strong?' asked Chandra.

'He is very powerful. He shines all night in the sky so that travellers can find their way,' said Deena.

'I'm glad I have a moon name,' said Chandra.

'No more stories,' Deena said. 'Look, here are our first customers!'

'How much are you selling your flowers for?'
asked Mr Gautam from the big hotel.

'They are five rupees a bunch,' said Deena.

They started to sell their flowers.

Every day Chandra and Deena picked blossoms
and took them down to the market square. By the
end of the week, Deena's bead purse was full.

'Is it enough for the deposit?' said Chandra.

'We have four hundred rupees,' said Deena,
counting out the coins. 'We need one hundred more.'

Chandra watched
the man selling the
solar *tukis*. People were
queuing up to buy them.
'Will you save one for
us?' she begged. The
man looked at all the
people waiting.

'I'll keep one for half
an hour,' he said.

'Chandra, stay here. I'll run home and fetch Father,' said Deena.

Chandra sat down next to the man and watched. Soon there were just two lamps left. Still Father and Deena didn't come.

By the time Deena and Father came hurrying to the stall, Chandra was in tears. 'All the *tukis* are sold,' she sobbed.

'Will you have some more soon?' Father asked the vendor.

'Not for a while,' said the man. Then Chandra spotted the demonstration *tuki*.

'What about that one?' she asked.

'I need that one to show people,' the man said.

Chandra raced back to the flower tins and grabbed the rest of the flowers.

'Please let us buy it!' she cried. 'You can have these. Please! Our baby brother has a bad cough and this lamp will help him!'

The man nodded. He picked up the last *tuki* and handed it to Chandra.

When the sun went down, Father carried the solar *tuki* inside. He turned it on and the room was filled with a soft yellow glow. He said a prayer of thanks to the sun god Surya for giving them light. They ate supper in the warm glow of the lamp.

After supper, Deena got out her school books and
Mother took out her sewing. Chandra went to bed.

As she curled under the covers,
the moon cast silver pools of light onto her quilt.
'Thank you, Chandra,' Chandra said to the moon.
In a corner of the room, the solar *tuki* shone over
Deena's head as she read her book. Akash slept,
wrapped in his quilt, breathing quietly.
'Thank you, Surya,' whispered Chandra to the
magic light.

Nepal

Mountains

Nepal is a long, thin country that lies along the southern slopes of the Himalaya Mountains, with India to the south and China to the north. The Himalayas are the highest mountains in the world — eight of the world's ten tallest mountains are in Nepal, including the highest point on Earth, Mount Everest. From the mountains flow rivers that bring water to many thousands of people in the fertile valleys and plains of Nepal and north India.

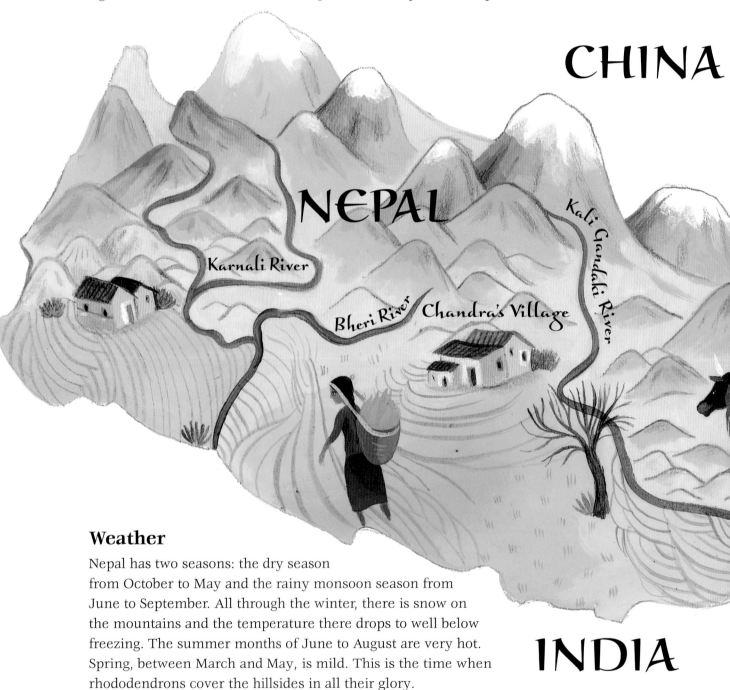

CHINA

NEPAL

Karnali River

Kali Gandaki River

Bheri River

Chandra's Village

Weather

Nepal has two seasons: the dry season from October to May and the rainy monsoon season from June to September. All through the winter, there is snow on the mountains and the temperature there drops to well below freezing. The summer months of June to August are very hot. Spring, between March and May, is mild. This is the time when rhododendrons cover the hillsides in all their glory.

INDIA

Rivers

Some Nepali rivers are named for their qualities, such as the fast-flowing Bheri, which is one of the best rivers in the world for rafting and kayaking. Other rivers have religious meaning. Legend says that one of Lord Vishnu's lovers, Gandaki, begged always to be with him, so he turned her into the Kali Gandaki River and he became the Salagrama stones that are still found on the river's banks.

Most Nepali people live in villages in the foothills of the Himalayas. In the middle of the country, in a large bowl-shaped valley, lies Kathmandu, which is the capital of Nepal and its largest city.

The Nepali Flag

The Nepali flag is the only flag in the world that is not quadrilateral. Instead, it is shaped like two overlapping pennants — the small, fluttering triangular flags that ancient Nepali warriors carried into battle and the prayer flags that Nepali people tie to posts and trees. The flag is a complex mathematical shape and the geometric rules of how to draw it are written into Nepal's laws.

The two triangles show how Nepal is made up of high mountains and how, after years of battles between warring tribes, the country was formed as one kingdom. The red background and white sun represent the courage of the Nepali people, and the blue border shows their love of peace.

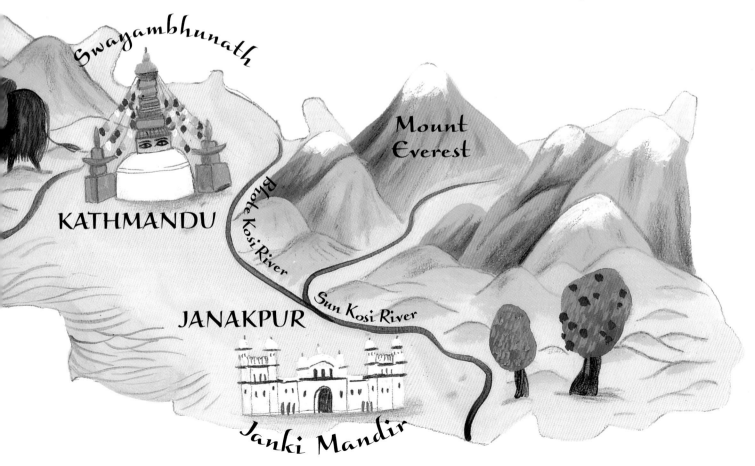

Religion

Many Nepali people are Hindus. Hindus believe there is no one special way to lead your life, that there are 'many paths, one truth'.

They believe that there is one true god, the supreme spirit, called Brahman. Brahman is the god of creation and the universe. Brahman contains everything: creation and destruction, male and female, good and evil, movement and stillness.

There are many Hindu gods and goddesses. Each of them represents a different form of the true god, Brahman.

Most Hindus choose to pray to one special god or goddess, like Krishna or Lakshmi, who is important to them.

Chandra is the god of the moon. He is handsome and young and rides his chariot across the sky every night, pulled by seven white geese. Girls and boys are named after him.

Surya is the name of the sun and of the sun god. Many Hindus perform sun salutations at dawn to honour Surya. In pictures, artists paint him golden-red, holding lotus flowers.

Rhododendrons

The national flower of Nepal is the red rhododendron.

Rhododendrons bloom in March and April, adding astonishing colours to the hillsides as spring begins. Lower down the mountains, the blooms are rich red, but on the higher slopes, the flowers become pink and then white.

In winter, fresh rhododendron leaves make good fodder for farm animals. The wood from the larger trees is used for furniture, house beams and garden fencing. The flower petals can be eaten; they contain a few drops of honey, delicious for sucking out. The dried petals make healthy herbal teas.

People and Work

Many Nepali people work as farmers. They grow tea, corn, wheat, sugarcane and root crops. The farmers dig terraces for their crops into the steep mountainsides. They also keep buffalo and goats for meat, and cows for milk.

Most people in Nepal are Pahari. Pahar means hill and many Pahari people live in the hills and mountains of the Himalayas.

The Sherpas are the most famous Nepali people and their home is in the central and eastern Himalayas. Sherpas are famous for their elite mountaineering skills. There are no better leaders or guides to take expeditions across some of the country's most challenging terrain.

Beautiful landscapes, superb hiking trails and fast-flowing rivers for kayaking and rafting make Nepal more and more popular as a holiday destination. That means that tourism is now an important way of earning money in Nepal.

Markets

The street markets of Nepal are very busy and colourful. The traders sell from wooden stalls or woven baskets set out on the streets. You can find almost anything at these outdoor markets: fresh fruit and vegetables, cakes, spices, clothing, juice, farm animals, jewellery, pots, pans and, of course, flowers like Chandra and Deena's rhododendron bouquets.

The herbs and spices of Nepal give the market a wonderful smell. *Tulsi*, which the girls buy for Akash, is also known as holy basil. It is a scented, woody herb that is often used to treat coughs.

Most families in Nepal buy fresh fruits and vegetables every day and the market is a very important part of their lives. People travel long distances along difficult roads to get to market. Farmers may carry what they want to sell in wicker baskets balanced on bamboo poles across their shoulders. Women carry pots and baskets on their heads.

The money in Nepal is the Nepali rupee. There are one hundred paise in every Nepali rupee, just as there are one hundred pence in every pound.

Health

Because so many of the villages in Nepal are in the hills and mountains, it is hard for many Nepali people to go and see doctors or nurses. They might have to walk a long way to reach the nearest clinic and often there are no proper roads. People might use traditional treatments to help them get better: herbs and special chants and prayers.

Solar *Tukis*

Most of the people who live in Nepal do not have electricity in their homes. Their only light comes from kerosene lamps called *tukis*. These lamps are very dim and the kerosene is very smelly. The fumes are unhealthy, as well as bad for the environment. The other danger is that *tukis* can easily overbalance, which can start a house fire.

Solar *tukis* are simple to use and light to carry. They are a safe and sustainable use of energy. They absorb energy from the sun during the day and use the energy to power light bulbs at night. Solar *tukis* seem expensive to buy, but they cost no more than a year's worth of kerosene fuel for an ordinary *tuki*.

How to Make a Pizza Box Solar Oven

Discover the power of solar energy yourself by building a solar oven. Solar ovens are great for making cheesy bread or chips. Simply put cheese on a slice of bread or chips and watch how the sun makes it turn gooey and crispy. Remember to use oven gloves when taking your food out of the oven.

You will need:
- pizza box
- craft knife or sharp kitchen knife
- aluminium foil
- tape
- plastic wrap (or two plastic zip-lock bags)
- dark paper (black is best!)
- newspaper
- ruler

1 Draw a square on the lid of the pizza box, 5cm from each side. Get a grown-up to help you cut along three sides with a knife to make a large flap on the top of the box — don't cut the side at the back of the box. Fold the flap up along the fourth line so that it stands up. (It helps to hold a ruler along the back of the fold line to crease it the first time.)

2 Cover the bottom of the flap with aluminium foil, folding the foil up over the edges and onto the top of the flap. Tape down the edges on the top to stick the foil in place. The foil will reflect the sun's rays into the box.

3 Stretch the clear plastic wrap (or plastic bags that are cut into long rectangles) over the square hole and secure it tightly around the edges with tape. This should create an airtight window that lets light and heat into the box.

4 Next, open the box. Using your dark paper, line the bottom of the box. The dark paper will absorb the sun's heat. Black is the best, because the colour black absorbs more heat from the sun than other colours.

5 Roll up the sheets of newspaper and line the edges of the bottom of the box. Tape them down so that they surround the cooking area. This will help your oven keep in more heat.

6 Your solar oven is complete! For the best results, try it out on a sunny day between 11am and 3pm when the sun is strongest. Be sure to keep the flap open at an angle that reflects as much sun as possible into the box — use a ruler to hold it up.

Visit www.barefootbooks.com for more activities.